Published by Creative Education
123 South Broad Street, Mankato, Minnesota 56001
Creative Education is an imprint of The Creative Company

Designed by Stephanie Blumenthal
Production Design by The Design Lab

Photos by: Archive Photos, Allsport Photography,
Anthony Neste Photography, Focus on Sports, FPG International,
Janine Pestel Photography

Library of Congress Cataloging-in-Publication Data

Bach, Julie S., 1963–
Jeff Gordon / by Julie Bach
p. cm. – (Ovations)
Summary: Describes the life of the NASCAR driver,
from his childhood through his current career.
ISBN 0-88682-939-9

1. Gordon, Jeff, 1971– –Juvenile literature. 2. Automobile racing
drivers–United States–Biography–Juvenile literature. [1. Gordon, Jeff,
1971– 2. Automobile racing drivers.] I. Title. II. Series: Ovations
(Mankato, Minn.)
GV1032.G67B33   1999
796.72'092–dc21   97-41467

2   4   6   8   9   7   5   3

JEFF

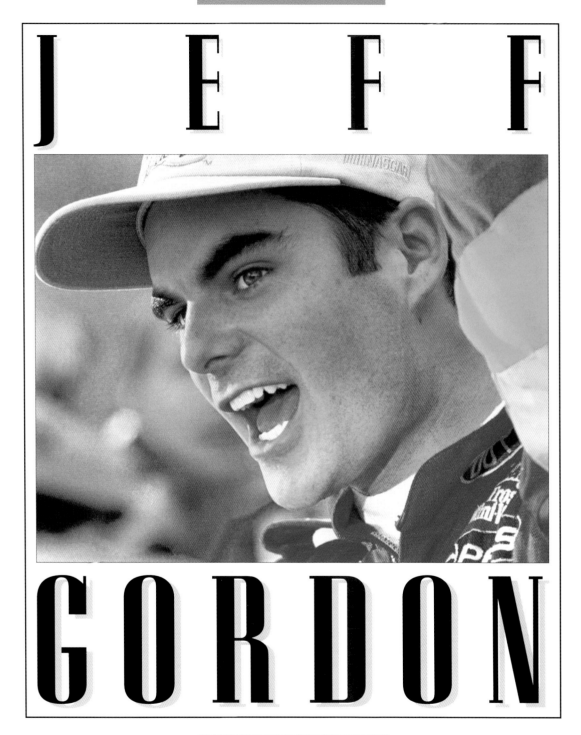

GORDON

BY JULIE BACH

Creative Education

REFLECTIONS

Jeff Gordon, a young stock car racer, laps the track at the Daytona Motor Speedway. He's in third place behind two of the best drivers in racing—Bill Elliot and Dale Earnhardt. His teammates, Terry Labonte and Ricky Craven, are close behind him.

Suddenly Jeff, known as "The Wonder Kid," makes a move for first place. He charges low into Turn 2 and comes back up into the middle of the track as he enters the straightaway. He survives a sideswipe from Dale's car and moves on. Two other drivers clip Dale, spinning him out of the race.

Ahead of Jeff, Bill races toward the finish with just 11 laps to go. But Jeff's got an idea. He contacts his

teammates by radio. "Terry," he says, "it would be pretty neat if we could get our three cars by Elliot." Terry replies, "Yeah, that'd be neat. I'll be with you." Ricky chimes in, "I'm going with you."

On Turn 1, Jeff plunges left and his teammates veer right. Bill Elliot doesn't know who to block and ends up being left behind by all three. Jeff takes first place in the race, and his teammates take second and third. Later, in the winner's circle, Jeff explains that he won the race for owner Rick Hendrick. A few weeks earlier, the team's owner had been diagnosed with leukemia, a deadly blood disorder. "It didn't matter which of us finished first, second, or third," Jeff said, "so long as we finished 1-2-3 for Rick."

Jeff Gordon's desire to win—not only for himself but for others—is the distinguishing mark of this up-and-coming champion. Many people believe that Jeff has what it takes to be the best stock car racer in history.

In spite of his success, Jeff Gordon never forgets the people who have helped make him the star he is today: his crew and his fans.

EVOLUTION

For a champion race car driver,
Jeff Gordon is young—he was
born on August 4, 1971, in Vallejo,
California—but he's been racing cars
longer than most people his age have
been driving.

At age five, his parents bought
him two go-carts. Jeff, whose full
name is Jeffrey Michael Gordon, took
to the cars immediately, and it was his
idea to enter races. "Once I realized,
'Hey, I can control this car,' I was
fascinated by it," Jeff recalled. By
the time he was eight years old, he
was racing quarter-midgets nearly
every weekend, and winning most
of the time. He often won against
kids more than twice his age.

His mother, Carol, had
divorced when Jeff was one year old
and soon remarried John Bickford, an
auto parts maker. They both supported

Jeff's interest in racing, even though the sport could be dangerous. "We were always trying to prepare for the next opportunity—that would be the way to say it," John remembered. "I think all parents have a certain level of concern, but if he chose skydiving I'd be more worried than racing."

At age 11, Jeff won the quarter-midget nationals. He seemed destined to race. But by age 14, Jeff became impatient with racing other teenagers. He knew he was good enough to race against adults, but California rules did not allow that. The family faced a decision. His parents felt that Jeff's racing career was important, so they moved to Pittsboro, Indiana, where racing rules were not as strict and Jeff could be closer to the sport's action. Bickford gave up his manufacturing business in California and dedicated himself to Jeff's career.

In Indiana, life was far from easy. The family had no full-time income and lived partially off Jeff's winnings. "[We] slept in pickup trucks and made our own parts," said John Bickford. "I think Jeff is misunderstood by people who think he was born to rich parents and had a silver spoon in his mouth."

Before he was old enough to have an Indiana driver's license, Jeff had won three sprint car championships. He competed in sprint car

Whether he's preparing for the race, on the course in his Dupont stock car, or getting advice from his crew, Jeff is all business when he's at the track.

races abroad and eventually won the United States Auto Club (USAC) midget title in 1990. Then, that summer, just before his 19th birthday, his stepfather suggested that he attend the Buck Baker stock car driving school at Rockingham, North Carolina. At Rockingham, when Jeff took his first lap in a stock car, he fell in love with the sport.

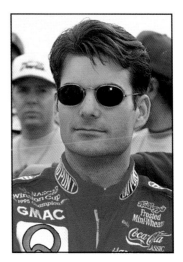

Stock car racing is organized by NASCAR, which stands for the National Association of Stock Car Auto Racing. Stock cars are passenger cars converted into race cars. They're different from Indy cars, which are smaller and faster. Stock car racing traces its roots to Prohibition in the 1920s, when daring young men drove back-country roads in the South delivering whiskey, which at the time was illegal. These drivers altered their cars to be able to outrun the authorities. On weekends, they got together at dirt tracks to see whose car was faster.

Because of its origins, stock car racing has for a long time been mainly a Southern sport. Jeff entered the rink as an outsider. Not only was he from California, but he hadn't grown up around NASCAR. He had, however, won 600 races by the time he climbed inside a stock car. Those who knew

him best had little doubt that he would
handle stock cars with equal success.

Jeff started out in the Busch
Grand National series. (Busch Grand
National is to stock car racing what
the AAA league is to professional
baseball.) There he won Rookie of the
Year. He also continued competing
in the USAC and won the Silver
Crown championship in Indy-
type sprints in 1991. Still,
his heart was with stock
car racing, and in 1992
he turned his full atten-
tion to the Busch series.

THE BIG BREAK

In March 1992, Jeff competed in a
Busch Grand National race at Atlanta
Motor Speedway. He was driving the
number 1 Carolina Ford, owned by
Bill Davis. Rick Hendrick, a car
dealership owner, was there scout-
ing new prospects. Rick watched
Jeff beat Dale Earnhardt and Harry
Gant, both of whom were veteran
drivers. Rick later said, "I thought,
'Man, that guy's gonna wreck; you
can't drive a car that loose.'"

Rick was so impressed with
Jeff's racing abilities, however, that
he told his general manager to sign
"The Kid" to a contract, whatever it
took. Rick wanted Jeff to race in the
Winston Cup series, the major leagues
of stock car racing.

J eff knew enough about NASCAR to know that a contract with
Rick Hendrick was a ticket to the big time. Rick was one of the
wealthiest stock car owners and had the resources to put together a winning
team. Jeff agreed to a long-term contract and began racing Rick's number
24 Dupont Chevrolet. Jeff drove his first Winston Cup race at the very end
of the 1992 season. He was just 21.

As Jeff expected, Rick provided him with the best technical crew
a driver could hope for. At the head of the crew was Ray Evernham, a talented engineer who still treats Jeff like a younger brother. The rest of the
crew, a group of engineers and mechanics, named themselves the Rainbow
Warriors. Jeff's crew can change all four tires and fill the gas tank in 20
seconds. With such top-notch people to back him, Jeff knew there would
be nothing to stop him from winning the Winston Cup races.

At the beginning of the 1993 season, Jeff was ready, and so were
the Rainbow Warriors. He started the year by winning one of the Twin 125s
at Daytona. These two races are NASCAR's version of the first game of

*Jeff doesn't mind
mingling with the
competition before
a race, but he shows
them no mercy once
he hits the track to
bring the Dupont
team another victory.*

WINNER
1997

spring training. He was the youngest driver ever to win a Twin 125.

After the race, a Winston model named Brooke Sealey presented Jeff with the winner's trophy. Brooke and Jeff had noticed one another around the tracks, but NASCAR had a rule stating that models and drivers could not date. But Jeff wasn't going to let that stop him. "He came up to me at Daytona and he asked me to go eat lunch." Brooke recalled with a laugh. "His voice was quivering; he was real nervous." Their first date began a secretive courtship. Brooke and Jeff met on the sly in restaurants where other racers didn't go. Their relationship was so secretive that friends began to wonder why such a handsome guy and such a beautiful girl never had dates.

A year later, Brooke ended her commitment as a Winston model. That evening, in a French restaurant in Daytona, Jeff proposed. Brooke accepted. "She had me wrapped around her finger from the first date," Jeff admitted. They married in 1994 and moved into a four-bedroom home on a lake north of Charlotte, North Carolina.

The year that Jeff and Brooke secretly dated, Jeff was named the 1993 Winston Cup Rookie of the Year. He finished second in NASCAR's longest race, the Coca-Cola 600 at Charlotte Motor Speedway, and he finished 14th in the point standings. It was the best showing by a

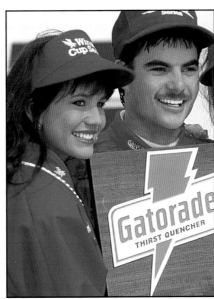

Jeff's career in NASCAR has led him not only to numerous victories, but also to his wife Brooke, opposite, a former track model Jeff met at a Winston Cup race.

rookie NASCAR driver in years. Stock car racing fans knew that they had a future champion on their hands.

The following year Jeff won the Coca-Cola 600. Then, in August, he won the first NASCAR race ever run at the Indianapolis Motor Speedway. The race was called the Brickyard 400, and it drew attention because NASCAR had never run a race at Indy before. After winning $613,000—the largest Winston Cup purse at that time—Jeff and Brooke quietly celebrated by ordering a pineapple pizza from room service. He finished the season an incredible eighth in points.

Jeff's third year in Winston Cup racing was a big one. He started the 1995 season slowly with a poor run in the Daytona 500, but then won races at Rockingham, Atlanta, and Bristol. By the middle of the season he had piled up so many wins that people were starting to speculate about him clinching the championship.

It seemed unlikely that such a young driver could come almost out of nowhere to win the biggest title in stock car racing, but Jeff was determined. He kept his cool through the rest of the season, winning race after race, until he was 300 points ahead of second-place Dale Earnhardt. The last few races of the season were hardly necessary. Jeff was so far ahead of all

Although Jeff is the one who receives the checks and trophies, he credits much of his success to hard-driving competitors like Dale Earnhardt, opposite left, who are constantly pushing him to excel, and to the crew that prepares his car for every race.

the other drivers that from September on the championship was in the
bag. After the final race of the year, in Atlanta, Jeff was cheered by thou-
sands of fans who had watched his season with amazement. At age 24,
he had won stock car racing's most important title.

Earnhardt was baffled by this "Wonder Boy," and a little
needled at his success. Dale had earned the nickname
"Intimidator" by driving aggressively on the tracks. If he would have
won the Winston Cup in 1995, he would have broken a record by winning
it eight times. When someone asked how he felt about Jeff winning the
cup, the older man groused that when Jeff accepted his honors at the
awards banquet, they would "probably serve milk instead of champagne."

Jeff took the older man's teasing in stride, and even decided
to play a little gag. When Jeff accepted the trophy award at the Waldorf-
Astoria Hotel in New York, he had a waiter bring him a silver champagne
bucket. Jeff pulled a bottle from the bucket, poured himself a glass of
milk, and toasted Dale Earnhardt, who sat grinning in the first row.

M ORE THAN A WINNER

Jeff's sense of humor is one of the qualities that make him a superstar in the world of stock car racing and a celebrity around the country. He's a clean-cut man who enjoys talking to people and meeting his fans. Jeff has his own Web site and has joined in on-line chats with fans around the world.

Racing cars is a career that has brought Jeff a great deal of wealth and fame, and he's happy to share his good fortune with others. Partly because of Rick Hendrick's struggle with leuke-mia, and partly because crew chief Ray Evernham has a son with the disease, Jeff makes several contributions a year to the Leukemia Society of America and acts as a spokesperson to raise awareness about the disease. Through a program called "Racing for a Rea-son," Jeff's team encourages fans to fight leukemia.

J eff also donates time and money to Easter Seals and the Make-A-Wish Foundation. He spends time at children's hospitals and volunteers for the Turner Adventure Learning program, helping school children learn math and science skills. Fans see Jeff making public service announcements urging people to use seat belts, practice watersport safety, and avoid smoking cigarettes.

Jeff's desire to help others is nurtured by the Bible studies he at-tends with his wife. Brooke, who was

Equally amazing as Jeff's success on the NASCAR track is the way he has handled fame at such a young age. To the dismay of his competition, Jeff's best years as a driver are likely still ahead of him.

raised in a family with strong religious beliefs, places Bible verses on the steering wheel or dashboard of Jeff's car each race day. Jeff says his religious beliefs help him keep things in perspective: "God comes first, family second, and racing third," he explained. "I try to keep the things I do morally in line with the way I live my life."

As a NASCAR champion, Jeff has an exceptionally busy life. The racing season extends from February through November. Jeff and Brooke travel together to all the races, which are run on Sundays. They usually arrive in town on Friday nights and spend some time together before the busy day of practices and qualifying laps on Saturdays. On Sundays, Brooke watches from the stands. "When he gets in a race car," she said, "I want to be with him."

1997 DAYTONA 500 WINNER
THE HARLEY EARL AWARD

Jeff likes to be available to his fans as much as possible. He signs autographs wherever he goes, even when he and Brooke are out at the local bowling alley. He's been on the "Late Show with David Letterman" several times, and even had a cameo appearance in the FOX-TV movie *Steel Chariots*, which aired in September 1997.

Off the race track, Jeff enjoys shooting hoops with Brooke in their driveway, jet-skiing, and playing computer games. He also scuba dives and plays golf. When he's not on the race track, he drives a Chevrolet Blazer. He also owns a classic 1934 Ford.

GAINING RESPECT

After Jeff's 1995 Winston Cup championship, the world of NASCAR was watching to see what he would do in 1996. As it turned out, Jeff didn't win the championship again that year, but he had a great season and provided some excitement for the fans.

One of Jeff's teammates on the Hendrick team, Terry Labonte, is a talented driver as well. By the end of the 1996 season, Jeff and Terry had been in a race for points. Jeff had won 10 races, but coming into the final race of the season at Atlanta Motor Speedway, Jeff was trailing Terry by 47 points. If Terry finished eighth or better, he would clinch the title.

Jeff Gordon relies on his crew, whose tireless work both before and during a race often determines the Dupont team's success.

"We just have to go out and give it all we've got and hope for the best," Jeff said before the race. That's what he and the Rainbow Warriors did. Terry finished fifth and took the Winston Cup championship for 1996. Jeff placed second in points.

Jeff bounced back at the beginning of the 1997 season by winning the Busch Clash and the Daytona 500. As the season progressed and Jeff won more races, people began to talk of the "Wonder Kid" winning another championship. But by now, Jeff wasn't such a "kid" anymore. His talent and expertise on the race track were taken as a matter of course. The older NASCAR drivers knew they had to take Jeff seriously if they intended to beat him.

By the end of the season, Jeff had racked up 10 wins and was 77 points ahead of second-place Mark Martin. Dale Jarrett was a close third. Going into the final race of the season, the NAPA 500 at Atlanta Motor Speedway, Jeff needed to finish 18th or better to win the championship.

The weekend of the race started out badly for Jeff. First he wrecked his primary car in Saturday morning's practice. That left him in his backup car with no time for practice and no laps on the car. Later, trying to qualify his backup car, he slipped going around a turn and ended up starting 37th in the field, his worst start all year. But in spite of these troubles, Jeff Gordon and his Rainbow Warriors ran a solid race and finished in 17th place. Jeff brought his Chevrolet Monte Carlo to a stop at the end of the race, climbed onto the roof of the car, and began jumping up and down for joy. At age 26, he had won his second Winston Cup Championship. In five seasons, he had tallied 29 career victories on the NASCAR circuit, 20 in the last two years.

Jeff has been so successful in NASCAR that it's hard to believe he's been racing stock cars for such a short time. He seems to enjoy the sport more with each passing season. "A lot of things we're doing are still fun and new," he said. "The sport's growing, so that part of it is fun. I enjoy it. Right now, I wouldn't change a thing."

Jeff has had his share of wrecks in the dangerous sport of stock car racing, but he has always bounced back in high style.

VOICES

On his career:

"I'm your very typical quarter-midget kid who made it to the big time."
Jeff Gordon

"[He's got] tremendous self-confidence, a relentless desire to succeed, and a surprising degree of humility."
John Bickford, Jeff's stepfather

"I've had to learn a lot of things very quickly, and I try to learn from my mistakes. You've got to fight hard to win a championship."
Jeff Gordon

"I hear people say there's a natural ability, a God-given talent to be able to drive a race car. I don't know if I agree. Having done it since the age of five, it's routine."

> *Jeff Gordon*

"The laps he drove when he was six or seven years old, he's still applying them."

> *John Bickford, on Jeff's long career*

"I'd like to win at every track we race on. Winning never gets old."

> *Jeff Gordon*

On Fear:

"You can't live your life worrying. I'm more afraid of dying walking down the sidewalk than I am driving a race car, because I know if I do it in a race car, it will be doing something I love to do."

Jeff Gordon

"Sometimes I get excited, but Jeff can take it—he's so calm. He stays calm; I try to stay calm. He does a better job of it."

Ray Evernham, Rainbow Warriors crew chief

On His Family:

"We do everything together. She goes with me to all the races. I've got my own airplane now, so it makes it much easier for us to do things together. I can't think of anything we don't do together."

Jeff Gordon about Brooke

"If it hadn't been for my stepdad, I wouldn't be where I am today."

Jeff Gordon

He may go it alone on the track, but Jeff can always rely on the support of his crew in the pit and his wife, Brooke, in the stands.

ON LIFE AS A CAR RACER:

"There isn't a day that goes by that something about racing isn't done. That's just my life. I could be doing something every hour of every day and not fulfill all the opportunities that are out there. And it's exciting! I feel very blessed to have that opportunity."

Jeff Gordon

"In a world where a lot of sports heroes have rainbow hair and earrings and are getting locked up and have drug problems, I think he's good for our sport."

Ray Evernham

"Out of the car, he's like a junior high school kid. But inside the car, he's a fierce competitor. Whatever it takes to win, that's what he does."

Kyle Petty, race car driver

Jeff Gordon's youthful exuberance and charisma—not to men-tion his success—has made him an appealing star in NASCAR.

○N PROFESSIONAL RACING:

"Jeff and his team know they can't just go down there and ride around and win the championship. They have to race, and when you have to race, anything can happen."

Dale Jarrett, driver

"This is a tough sport—this isn't croquet. It's Winston Cup racing and it's about doing the things you've got to do to win. It's every man for himself."

Jeff Burton, driver

"You can't show that you're scared. You can't show any weakness."

Jeff Gordon

Huge checks, victory celebrations, autograph signings—just another day in the life of Jeff Gordon.

FROM THE COMPETITION:

"I sure would have liked to win the last one here at North Wilkesboro, but I burned up my tires trying to run Jeff down."

> *Dale Earnhardt on placing second after Gordon in the Tyson Holly Farms 400*

"It was great racing, the way it should be in Winston Cup. Me and Jeff raced each other those last few laps real close, but real clean."

> *Ernie Irvin, celebrating his Miller 400 win over Gordon*

"All we can do is go out and do our very best every week. The 24 car [Gordon] is going to be hard to catch."

> *Mark Martin on Gordon's 1997 105-point lead*

ABOUT JEFF GORDON:

"Jeff is the hardest working athlete I've ever seen. Every second he has something booked."

Monica Seles, tennis star

"He was so sweet, so down to earth."

Brooke Gordon, on her first impression of Jeff

"What I found was a mature young guy who was kind of humble—a little bashful."

Rick Hendrick,
on first meeting Jeff

Jeff's talent, work ethic, and down-to-earth attitude about success make it likely that the competition will continue to see the backside of the Dupont stock car for years to come.

OVATIONS